GREYHUFFINGTON

liam

THE **EISENBERG EFFECT** BOOK FOUR
THE **DOMINO EFFECT** PREQUEL

and making sure that I properly prepare you
for what is to unfold within the pages of this
book.

violence
sexual assault
drug addiction
suicide
homicide
miscarriage/child loss
child abuse
emotional abuse

PAPERBACKS
HARDCOVERS
SHORT STORIES
AUDIOBOOKS
MERCH
AND MORE...

instagram.com/greyhuffington

LET'S GET SOCIAL

Instagram:

Grey Huffington
(Cover reveals, releases, etc)
Instagram.com/greyhuffington

HuffingtonHQ
(News, updates, etc —headed by Team Huffington)
Instagram.com/huffingtonhq

TikTok:

Grey Huffington
(Vlogs, updates, promotional images/videos, etc — headed by Team Huffington)
TikTok.com/@greyhuffington.com

Pinterest:

Grey Huffington
(Inspiration, quotes, snippets, visuals, boards, lifestyle, etc —headed by Team Huffington)
https://pin.it/695pEOV9m

CONTENTS

GREY HUFFINGTON

liam

THE **EISENBERG EFFECT** BOOK FOUR
THE **DOMINO EFFECT** PREQUEL

ONE

liam

"OPEN UP, SON," I instructed for the hundredth time to a sleepy and hardly interested Laike.

The expensive ass high chair that his mother had purchased him, specifically for my office since it was where he was most often, did little to support his wobbly neck. After a few rounds of airplanes, numbers, and alphabets, my 6-month-old was pooped.

As much as I wanted to keep him awake another thirty minutes or so as I prepared for our departure, I knew he wouldn't last. I'd underestimated his exhaustion and stuck around the office a bit too long.

Hauling him around in his sleep and having to wake him every half hour to exit my office, journey home, and make it inside the house wasn't in my plans for him, but there was no way around it, now. I gnawed the inside of my jaw, disgusted with my miscalculation and future disruptions. Hadn't it been such a special day for his mother and me, I wouldn't mind sticking around the office for another hour or two while he rested. However, tonight wasn't one of those normal nights.

Fuck. I wanted my boy to enjoy the nap he deserved, but it was nearly impossible.

"One more bite," I encouraged him.

His eyes popped open as I stuffed the homemade apple, peach, and mango sauce into his mouth. Like the champion he was, Laike, the youngest of my two boys, swallowed every drop.

"That's it, big boy!"

My cheer startled him though it was low and light. His hands flew into the air, knocking the spoon from my hand. It landed in the bowl of baby food, causing it to splatter. A chunk landed on my shirt.

"Shit," I hissed, pulling my shirt from my chest.

Instinctively, I lowered my head and quickly swiped the pasty mixture off the black fabric with my tongue. The fruitiness of it was pleasant to the taste, causing me to silently thank God. I'd run into some shitty concoctions that my wife had made for both Luca and Laike, making me regret putting that shit in my mouth without thinking twice.

Thankfully, the stain that I'd anticipated hadn't settled or wouldn't be appearing. Cleanliness was the closest thing to Godliness and I was trying to get as close to that nigga as possible with the life that I led, otherwise. With children, sometimes it was a bit farfetched, but as much as I could, I remained as crisp and clean as fatherhood allowed.

With stretched legs, I rose from the seat in front of Laike's high chair and stretched every inch of my six-foot, four-inch frame. A far cry from a minuscule nigga, my large frame was a direct correlation between the pieces of my existence and everything in my world. There wasn't shit about me small.

Big pockets, big dick, big bank accounts,

big deals, big investments, big businesses, big bricks, big boats, big homes, big shipments, big checks, big everything.

I grabbed the wet cloth from the back of the chair and wiped Laike's face before cleaning the tray in front of him. His head bobbed up and down, slowly, as he fell deeper into his slumber. Too worried it would fall off if I didn't interfere, I hurried to put the towel away, unclamp the sides, and pull Laike out.

My hands rested underneath his underarms, giving me full control of his healthy frame. Just like his brother, he wasn't the size of the average baby. He was a chunk of meat with lengthy legs and a fat ass head. They'd gotten that shit from me.

"How much is it Luca?" My voice projected across the room, causing Luca's shoulders to slump and his head to bow. "Head up!"

"I don't know," he whined.

Without seeing his brown eyes, I knew they were sad. However, I didn't give a damn about them or those features that were probably sagging on his face. They wouldn't get him any closer to the answers he needed.

"Then keep trying until you find out. Start over."

"Dad," he pleaded, though he was aware that it had never and never would get him anywhere with me or in life.

"How many twenties make a hundred?" I asked my two-year-old.

"Five," he responded.

"How many hundreds make a thousand?"

"Ten."

"What's five times ten?"

There was a brief silence as Luca did the math to a problem he should've been familiar with in his head. I waited, impatiently, but I waited.

"You know this, Luca."

"Fifty."

"Start there. And, soon you'll have a total for all that shit in front of you," I told him as I got Laike situated in the portable crib in the corner of my office.

Luca had used the same one and still did if he grew tired in the office. It wasn't too often because he was always busy trying to learn more and do more around the place to help me out. I was appreciative, though he was mostly only just in my way. To keep him busy, I gave him simple tasks like counting the one hundred thousand dollars that had him frustrated by hand.

It gave me a chance to teach him my favorite subject while keeping him out of my hair while I worked. At only two years and a few months old, Luca was a little mathematician. In addition to my daily lessons at the office, whenever he was home, his mother was enhancing his skills with more standard procedures and learning processes. Personally, I preferred the hands-on approach. There was no greater teacher than experience.

"Can you help?"

"Why would I help someone who has it under control? You're a very smart boy, Luca. I know you can solve this simple problem."

"I know," he voiced, lowly and without much confidence.

That pierced my heart, causing me to respond with reassurance almost immediately.

"Listen, son," I said to him, walking over to where he was seated on the floor with loose bills all around him, "This might seem a like a really big task but it's not. It's really just a little chaotic. How about you start by organizing the bills? Hmmm? Twenties in one pile and hundreds in another. Then, it won't look like such a big task. You've counted more than this before, Luca. You've got this.

Okay?" I patted his shoulder before lifting his head. "Keep that up. Alright? Never let that fall."

"Okay."

"Now, I have to go take care of some business before we get out of here. I need you to keep an eye on your brother. He's over there in the crib asleep."

"Okay, Dad."

"Cheer up, son. If you have the correct number for me by the time I return, then you can have all of it."

"Everything?"

"Everything," I assured him, amused at his intelligence.

He was a very bright kid, but I didn't expect anything less coming from my wife and me. As much as we poured into each other and our businesses, we poured twice as much into our children. Neither of us could take all the credit. It was a joint effort and one that I was most proud of.

"Have you already counted this over here?" I pointed to the neatly stacked bills.

"Yes."

"How much is it, son?"

"48,200," he replied, squinting as he tried to remember the exact number.

"That's my boy," I exclaimed, clapping

my hands, loudly, to show my gratitude, "You don't have much longer to go. Hurry."

I started for the door of my office. The last thing I was worried about was Luca getting his count correct and adding one hundred thousand dollars to his savings account. He'd shown me time and time again that money was his favorite subject and no matter how hard the task, he managed to master it.

"I love you, dad," Luca expressed, trying to place the really big feelings he was dealing with.

"Beyond measures," I returned with a smile, stopping in my tracks to give him my undivided attention, briefly.

"Always?" He questioned.

Often confused as to when and why I switched my response, Luca made sure to point it out. *Always. Beyond measure.* Though they both had different meanings, they were registered under the same branch in my book. I loved my children wholly, widely, forever, and always. The love in my heart for them was beyond anything that anyone could ever measure.

It was immeasurable, inexplicable, and all-encompassing. It was as restricted as it was limitless. There were no boundaries and no burdens on this love. So, it didn't matter which response I chose, I meant them both.

"Beyond measures, today," I confirmed.

With a smile, he nodded in understanding.

"Be-und measrree," he repeated. It was one of the few words he was still trying to adapt to.

"Yeah, son. That."

Calm. I warned, resting my right hand on my chest. It swelled with pride and admiration and adoration and gratitude for the little being before me. I couldn't have asked for a better offspring.

And though Laike was only six months, he was making me proud, too. From ASL communication to blabbering small words like dada, baba, and Uc which meant Luca, he was surprising us every day of his presence on Earth. He'd been crawling since four and a half months and was learning to stand on his own, now. I'd give him another two months before he was running around the office and giving Luca hell.

The smile that lined my lips was quickly swiped from my face altogether the second I stepped on the other side of my office door. As I stepped forward and in the direction of the warehouse, I shed the pieces and parts of

9

me that were reserved for the two humans that were once swimming in my nutsack and the woman whose eggs I fertilized every chance I got. By the time I arrived in the cold, gloomy space, I'd removed every trace of the man I was two minutes prior – which was the time it took for me to journey the distance downstairs.

"Boss, he–," Courtney, one of the soldiers keeping watch over the package began, but was quickly cut off with a finger to my lips.

I was both uninterested and unconcerned with whatever it was he was about to say. The second I walked through the door, I knew the fate of the man in front of me who wore a weary, exhausted expression on his face. I commended him for his loyalty and unwillingness to speak about their operation or where they'd successfully stashed over $1.2 million worth of dope that rightfully belonged to me, hoping that I wouldn't notice the shipment shortage.

Before my team opened, broke down, or distributed a single brick, the job was to count, weigh, and calculate it. Then, count, weigh, and calculate that shit, again. And, then, count, weigh, and calculate that shit a final time.

Because the third time was a charm and it

always did the trick. Every single time, the load was short $1.2 million, in street currency, worth of white. *Unacceptable*. That number, no matter how small or large, was bound to end in death. It didn't matter if it was recovered or not, the fact that anyone on Earth imagined they could live peacefully this lifetime after stealing from me was comical.

Joey understood this. He knew that his life would end tonight whether he talked to us or not, which was why he'd chosen to stay quiet. What he didn't understand was that it wouldn't only cost him his life, but the life of everyone on his team, everyone they encountered the day my shit came up short, and everything that moved in his home – down to the dog.

The only exclusion in this situation was the elderly, women, and children because they had nothing to do with his operation. If there was an inkling that they were, their blood would be shed, too, without an ounce of guilt or regret on my end. Luckily for him, he didn't have either under his roof. A lousy father and husband, he didn't deserve to walk the same streets as me, anyway.

"Anything you wish to declare this evening?" I asked Joey as I removed the .40

caliber from my waistline and marveled at its beauty.

It was a gift from my wife. She'd taken it upon herself to customize and purchase it from a really good friend and my arms dealer. It was as beautiful as it was untraceable. Though she wasn't in any way involved in my operations, she was aware of them to a certain extent. Laura knew nothing and that's how I preferred it. Beyond a few business calls and an occasional late night, I didn't bring work home with me. When I walked through the door of our home, I was a husband and a father. That's where my credentials ended. Anything beyond that was irrelevant.

His silence was revealing. So was the look on his face. Guilt was heavy on his shoulders and weighing his facial features down. Saving us both time and energy, I removed the safety from my gun that was active any time I was around the boys and pointed it at his bloody temple. He couldn't open his eyes, which happened to be swollen shut, but I still wanted his undivided attention before I put him out of his misery.

"Aye," I called out to Joey, causing him to lift his head, "See you in hell dirty motherfucker."

BLAOW! The recoil of my .40 was serious, perfecting the flick of my wrist. I loved the bit of movement that it received when on the offering end of the handgun. It pushed the blood through my veins a lot faster and made my heart drum a bit harder.

"Get the message to everyone else in his crew and anybody that helped them pull this shit off. Nobody walks. And, before you kill them motherfuckers, find one willing to talk. Not everyone knows they're dying regardless. Find him and then find my work," I stated, calmly.

"Boss, you have a call on line one," someone yelled.

"I'm on my way. Take out the trash. Leave no trace. See you niggas next week."

"You're taking time off?" Courtney asked, already knowing the answer.

"Stop asking stupid ass questions, my nigga. Save your words for more promising conversations because what's going on in my world isn't one."

If he thought I'd be discussing my dealing or plans pertaining to anything outside of the moment we were facing, then he was a little dumber than I thought. He'd been working alongside me for the last eight years and each year, I wondered if he really knew me at all.

Because questions like the one asked had continued to arise.

However, I'd once concluded that it was our history that caused him to ask stupid shit hoping that one day I'd let him in a little more. He was sadly mistaken. There wasn't a nigga in my camp or any camp, for that matter, that I'd let into my head, heart, or personal life. It was strictly business, always had been, and always would be. Without another word, I walked through the warehouse, reaching the door to exit in mere seconds.

When I approached the conference room, Red was standing outside of it with his palm pressed against the speaker at the bottom. Anxiousness caused his eyes to bulge and his feet to tap against the cemented floor. Once I was within earshot, he began whispering.

"It's Hunter. He says everything is good but he wants to speak to you about something."

"Tell him I'll talk to him once my package is secure. Until then, I'm not wasting my time or breath."

"Sure thing, boss," he responded as I turned around and headed in the opposite direction.

TWO

liam

I WAS STILL above ground level, floating
from the firing of my gun. I could smell the
powder that came along with it. Surely
enough, there was residue on my fingers, but
I wasn't worried about it. My only concern
was coming down from the high I was on by
indulging in another form of euphoria.

I reached my bunker in two minutes. It
was just shy of my actual office and where I

went to clear my head. Once I scrambled the numbers on the lock and opened the door, the television screens immediately lit up, but there was one monitor in particular that held my interest. It was the one that revealed the events of my office through the camera installed at the top corner. It was my eyes when I couldn't physically see what was happening inside.

That's my boy. I marveled, watching as Luca counted the money that I'd tasked him with as I removed a joint filled with the finest buds from the tin on the table in front of me. While lighting it, I began counting the bills with my boy. In sections of one thousand, he organized them. I wasn't sure how many he had so far, but by the look of the tiny stack he had left to count, I'd say he'd at least created ninety-four.

As the joint I'd rolled in the thin white paper came to an end, so did Luca's frustration. The pure excitement on his face when he bundled up the money for his keeping led me to stand and put the small fire out at the end of the spliff. I reached into the pocket of my pants and removed a stick of gum before opening the bunker's door and exiting.

Upon my arrival, Luca's cheeks rose and his head bobbed up and down. His success was inevitable. I knew he could finish the job. Now, he was a believer, too. That was the point of it all and would forever be.

"$100,000."

"Which brings your savings up to what?"

"$326,000."

"What you gone do with all that money?" I chuckled, patting his chest as I got down to his size.

"Give it to my wife," he boasted, proudly just like his father. "And, my baby."

"You're two, Luca. What do you know about a wife or some babies? Who told you that shit, youngin'?"

"My father," he replied, confidently.

"That's right."

I had and I'd been telling him since day one that it was the move. There wasn't anything out in the streets for him. Settling down with a deserving woman and having children was the most rewarding thing I'd ever done in my life. No amount of money I made could compare. If Luca decided to follow my footsteps – which he made clear even at his young age – I'd be alright with that.

"I have to show mommy," he told me, bouncing up and down with a few bills in his hands.

"And, you will because that's where we're headed. It's time to go home."

I loved when our days concluded because it meant that I could finally rest my bones and see the woman that made my life better each and every day.

When Luca dropped a few bills and extended his arm, I imagined he was signaling that he wanted a hug. However, that wasn't the case. His tiny finger glided across the skin of my forehead and then he slowly pulled it back to inspect it. My eyes followed the trail, ending at the tip of his forefinger where the crimson liquid appeared.

"Traces," he uttered.

Joey's blood wasn't only on my hands, it was on my son's hands, too, now. I cradled his little fingers inside of mine and swiped them clean. He wasn't surprised when I scooped him up into my arms and we headed for the sink. If I showed up at my door with blood on my skin, although it was on my hands, Laura would deny my entry. She had done so one too many times for me to forget or take her for a joke.

"Can't leave those," I chuckled, reminding Luca that it was unacceptable.

liam + laura

WITH THE BOYS gathered in their car seats in the back of my Chevy, I crept into the driveway of our home. The absence of my wife's car was baffling, causing me to cut our commute inside in half. Laike clung to my chest as I opened the door for us all.

"Laura?" I called out.

To my surprise, she didn't respond with her usual cheer at the sound of the boys and me returning home. She, too, spent her days working at her daycare center, so she was just as happy to be home as we were each day. Today was different, though, I felt it the moment I pulled into the driveway.

Movement in another area of the house caused me to lower Laike onto the ground and push Luca behind me as I removed the same .40 caliber I'd just used from my waist. Whoever had the nerve to enter my home unannounced and unwelcomed hopefully understood it was their last night on earth. I'd bet my last dollar that my children and I remained unharmed. I didn't see things going any differently. Couldn't. It was us or nothing.

"Liam, is that you?"

The sound of Laura's mother's voice eased my worries.

"Uh," I stuttered as I struggled to put the gun away before she appeared at the threshold, "Yes ma'am. Where, uh... Where's Laura? She didn't mention not being home this evening."

"I know, sorry," she apologized as she came into plain view, "She wanted to surprise you. According to her, there are instructions on the bed in your room upstairs. You'll find out more about whatever she has planned there."

"Or you could just tell me," I expressed with a shrug.

"Oh, honey, I can't. Laura would kill me. Besides, she didn't give many details. She just asked if her father and I could get the babies this weekend."

"This weekend? All weekend?" I asked with a tilted head. The thought of being without my boys for more than twenty-four hours put a dent in my chest. I felt slightly short of breath when I tried picturing it.

"Oh, God. I've said too much already. Liam, please go upstairs before you get me into trouble."

"All weekend?"

"This is probably why she didn't mention it to you. She knew you'd find a way around not being with the boys for a prolonged period. But, trust me, they'll be fine."

"I don't doubt for a second that they will be. It's just throwing me for a loop. All weekend."

I couldn't stop repeating myself. I assume it was because I was trying to convince myself that I could make it through without my boys. It would possibly be the most difficult thing I'd ever done in life. Since the day each of them was born, they were glued to my hip.

Not even Laura had them for too long without me snatching them up. Every day, she mentioned having a baby girl so that she didn't have to deal with my shit and I couldn't wait to make good on my promise to knock her ass up until she gave us one.

"You deserve the break, Liam. Take it."

"I never asked for a break," I chuckled, sarcastically.

"But, take it, anyway. Go ahead, now. She's waiting for you."

The last thing I wanted to do was keep my wife waiting but neither did I want to leave my boys behind. I turned toward Luca and kneeled before him. His smile was like a dagger to the heart, because I knew that it

23

wouldn't remain after I explained to him what was about to happen.

"Luca, daddy, and mommy are going away for a few days. You'll be with your grandmother and grandfather. I need you to be a big boy and take good care of your brother, okay?"

His smile remained plastered on his face as he nodded his head and wrapped his arms around my neck.

"Okay, daddy," he responded as he pulled back.

To my surprise, he had taken the news much better than I'd imagined and much better than me. I was dying a slow death inside while he remained calm and collected. He'd taken too many pages from my book. It was making me proud and unwell simultaneously.

"Good. Good. Good."

I went to find Laike but he had already taken off to another part of the house. Knowing that I'd be going on an adventure attempting to find him, I cut my losses early and headed upstairs to shower. Whatever my wife had planned, it could at least wait until after I'd scrubbed the day's work from my body.

liam + laura

FEELING MUCH FRESHER AND FINALLY, up to standard, I slipped into my shirt. The shower had blessed me in ways that I didn't know were possible. The urgency to see Laura quickened my pace and got me out of the door within minutes, but not before grabbing the gift that I'd hidden for her last week. I'd been waiting on this day to come and it was finally here. I wanted to celebrate her in the best and worst ways.

The name of a hotel that we were both familiar with was scribbled on the envelope that Laura had left on the bed. I'd snatched it up on my way out because it held a very important piece of plastic that I'd be needing to get inside room 1210. Underneath the hotel, she'd written the room number as well.

Like a school kid waiting to see his crush the next morning, I could feel the eagerness rising in my chest. Though it wasn't often throughout the day that I did so, Laura kept me smiling. Tonight wasn't much different. If I froze the moment to take a look in the mirror, I was almost certain that my lips were aiming to touch my ears.

She did that for me. Always had. Whether it was butterflies in my stomach or flutters of the heart, Laura could make it happen. And, after four years of marriage, she had yet to reduce or put out the flame that had been sparked between us. I wasn't sure what she had planned for me, but whatever it was, I was already grateful for it and couldn't wait to show my appreciation by returning the favor.

It was a special day for her and all I wanted to do was celebrate her life and her love. She'd one-upped me, though, and beaten me to the punch. That was fine with me, because tomorrow, we'd be headed to somewhere hot and sandy since the children would be away from us for the weekend. I wanted to take advantage of the time we'd have alone although it wasn't time that I thought was necessary.

The minute I got some free time and close to a landline, I'd make some arrangements for us to fly over the waters to catch some sun, do a little shopping, and explore. I wanted to stuff my face with Laura's pussy until the skin wrinkled and threatened to fall off. If I had anything to do with it, tonight would be the night that we made our daughter. She and Laike being fifteen months apart didn't sound too bad. Not to me, at least.

At the sight of a young boy rushing toward my car, I clutched the .40 on the seat next to me. It wasn't until he got a bit closer that I realized he was a valet attendant. *Lucky you*, I thought. He didn't realize just how close to death he was. Dressed in black from head to toe, he could've easily been mistaken for a threat and gotten his ass blown off.

"Good evening, sir," he greeted me as I rolled down my window. My left hand moved in a circular motion until it was down far enough for me to hear him clearly and vice versa.

"What's up?"

"Nothing much, sir. Will you be staying with us for the night? Are you checking in? Do you need someone to grab your luggage? What year is this car? It's sweet."

"You asking questions like the fucking police, Brandon," I said, reading his name tag.

"Park my shit up front in the event of an emergency. Can you handle that for me?" I asked, slipping him a twenty dollar bill, "And, keep the keys underneath the front driver tire."

"Sure thing Mr?" He hesitated.

"Eisenberg."

"Sure thing, Mr. Eisenberg."

"Don't touch shit in there. Park it and get your ass out," I advised, "And, it's an 84."

"Oh, this the new one?"

"It is. Step back so I can get out."

"I've got that for you," he insisted.

"I don't need another man to open my door; If you can help it, don't open the door for another man, either. Let him pick up his own slack."

"It kind of comes with the job," he chuckled.

"Understood, but outside of it, handle your own and let them do the same."

"Got it."

I journeyed through the hotel doors, the lobby, and the partygoers who were gathered outside of the ballroom near the elevator. Once I was inside, I pushed my back against the corner furthest to the right and waited impatiently for the doors to close. Just as they began, in walked a woman wearing red.

My jawline clenched as my hand rose slightly to rest on the butt of my gun. Small spaces that included human and a lack of distance wasn't at all my cup of tea. However, the curves of her frame and the subtle smile that raised her lips slightly made it a lot less hard to withstand.

"Your floor?" Her voice was lacey and angelic, mesmerizing me at the sound of it.

Too preoccupied with my thoughts and the prayer that no one entered the cart with me had caused me to forget that I needed to press the number twelve if I wanted to move. Words chose to hide briefly before I stood straight and narrowed my frame. However, my limbs still occupied territory that wasn't exactly necessary. Something or someone had obviously given them an inkling that they were entitled to the free space around me because it happened every time. So, even with a narrowed frame, my presence was emphasized.

"Twelve," I stated, calmly, clearing my throat shortly after.

"Twelve it is," she replied, delighted and happy to help me reach my destination.

Fourteen. It was the second number she dialed on the pad. Mentally, I scribbled it in my notes as she turned toward me. In a fiery red dress, she was dazzling. It was as if she'd just stepped off a runway. With her dark skin and high cheeks, I wondered why I didn't see a boulder on her left hand. Had she been mine, she'd still be doing exercises to adapt to the weight of it.

"Well, don't you look mighty fine, tonight? Special occasion?"

I nodded, twice in theatric motion, and then much smaller, gentler ones followed. Her smile widened as a thought came over her. I didn't have to wonder what that must've been for long because it came right out.

"I'm Stacy," she introduced, pushing her hand forward for me to accept.

Respectfully, I declined.

"Fiancé?" She narrowed her eyes and said.

I shook my head from one side to the other.

"Homosexual?" She tossed out.

I couldn't help the chuckle that escaped me as I shook my head, again.

"Hmmm. I didn't think so either, but it didn't hurt to ask."

"Happily married," I answered the next question before she asked because I knew it was coming.

"Ummmm. Figures. That was my next question. Lucky, lucky girl," she scoffed while eyeing me from head to toe.

"I'm the lucky one," I confessed as the bell of the elevator dinged, letting me know that I'd made it to my destination – made it closer to my home, my healer, my happy place. *Laura*.

I stepped forward as Stacy slid over. She made just enough room for me to get by, secretly hoping that our bodies made contact in even the smallest way. She didn't have to say it for me to know. It was in her stance, the look of anticipation on her face, and the closeness she chose not to expand.

It was always good to know that I could still feel but there was no greater feeling than knowing that I already had what was rightfully mine. In my opinion and experience, there wasn't a woman on Earth that could go toe to toe with mine. Laura was made specifically for me as I was made specifically for her.

We meshed well together. She was my person and I was hers. There wasn't anyone or anything that could convince me otherwise or to fuck that up; not a curvy frame, vanishing waist, pretty face, sultry voice, or good conversation. No matter how appealing a prospect might've been, it was never enough for me to consider betraying the woman that held my heart, head, and balls in her hands.

I was hers to keep. She was stuck with me for life. My world was in her possession and it would stay that way until the end of time.

"Farewell, now," she said, finally removing the claws she'd sunk into me.

With a simple nod, I headed in the direction of room 1210. Just because I loved the power Laura reigned over me even when she wasn't around, I was going to fuck her a little harder tonight. Because it was truly a fucking shame.

Whistling, I made my way down the hallway. Room 1210 was a short distance. I dug in my pocket and retrieved the room key that my wife had left on our bed. In front of it was a pretty little velvet box that my hand glided across before I managed to pull the key out. I aimed it for the door, but before I had the chance to gain access, it was granted.

In a black lace number, Laura stood beside the door with it wide open; neither of us worried about anyone who happened to pass by because we didn't mind them seeing what had been made perfectly for me. Laura was mine, all mine. Her entire body had been in my mouth and I'd be damned if she wasn't the sweetest thing I'd ever tasted.

Though it wasn't my objective to treat or think of my wife as a personal possession, there was no denying the relationship. I truly believed that she was birthed for me and vice versa. There was no other way of putting it.

"I got you something," I rushed out, pulling the box from my pocket.

Her beauty was my source of anxiousness. She was the only one with the power to make my thoughts fog, my tongue stutter, and my heart rate increase tremendously. It was almost painful to think about. The things this woman did to me and the neurological influence she had on me were nearly pathetic, but I loved every bit of it – every bit of her.

"Happy birthday, Liam."

Her pearly white teeth sparkled as she smiled. *Still.* It warned my heart, although there was no use. I was in the presence of royalty and it acted as such. She was the queen of our castle and it was always a grand occasion when she was involved.

"I upgraded you–," I started, but was cut off by a finger to the lip.

"It's your birthday, not mine. Why do you do this every year, baby?"

The smile never left her face but her brows knitted and tried bonding in the center of her forehead.

"Because it's your world, Laura. I'm just blessed to be part of it," I explained for the hundredth time.

"Tonight and tomorrow night and the next one, it's your world. Please, baby, try your hardest not to think of me or what makes me happy, laugh, smile, or anything of the sort. For once, I'm begging you to think about yourself. You have my permission to be selfish."

"But, I don't wanna be, baby girl. When it comes to my heart and my head when you're involved, you know which one will win – always."

"But, Liam try, at least."

"I can do that. Now, are you going to let me inside or what?"

It wasn't until then that I realized we were still standing at the door.

"Only if you promise to keep an open mind and not worry about me, tonight."

"I promise," I lied.

It wasn't often that I did, especially not to Laura. However, I was willing to bend a little tonight. There was no way in hell she could've assumed that shit was happening, but if it made her feel better, I'd agree to it.

She widened the door to the suite she'd booked us for the night or however long she planned to hold me, hostage. I could feel my eyes as they grew larger than their sockets. Nothing in the world could've prepared me for the sight before me. Taken aback, I remained planted in the thick carpet of the hotel hallway.

"Aren't you going to come in?"

I couldn't. My feet wouldn't move. My astonishment left me immobile.

"Liam," she called out, softly, to get my attention. But, she already had it. Always did.

"Uh... Baby. What the fuck is this?" I asked as the words came to me.

My temporary delayed movements and speech had subsided. The whispers that came from my lips were loud and forceful, defeating the purpose. My perplexity was at an all-time high. Confusion plagued me as I stared at my beautiful wife questioning the thought process behind the decision she'd made without my consent or approval. And, as enticing as it might have been for some, it wasn't for me. Exciting, *slightly*. Appreciated, *somewhat*.

"You're thinking about me and how I'm going to feel, again."

"Always, Laura," I admitted.

"You don't like the surprise?" She sighed as her eyes grew sad, tugging on my heart-strings.

"I do. I really do. It's just... not like... *us*."

Her smile returned, "I know but tonight isn't about *us*. It's about you."

Laura reached forward and rubbed the front of my pants with her right hand. As soon as her fingers landed on my dick, it swelled. *Same shit. Different day.* I silently teased.

My obsession with my wife wasn't a secret. It was now part of my actual identity. Depending on one's beliefs, it was as beautiful as it was sickening. I watched as she closed the gap between us and wet her shiny lips with her tongue. *Tantalizing.*

"I want to watch you fuck her and then I want you to fuck me and then I want to watch her clean my cream from your dick," she whispered in my ear, in a low and lusty voice. "You think you can do that for me, daddy?"

Fuck.

"She's clean. I had her tested. We can have a lot of fun with her," she added.

It was obvious that Laura had planned this further in advance than I'd given her credit for. Even our safety was considered in her decision and I appreciated that.

"And, she's not connected to anyone. She's almost a saint... almost. I've had someone sitting on her for the last 4 weeks."

Her cautiousness was intoxicating. Laura protected everyone in her castle. It was in her nature. Her protective instincts didn't end with her cubs. It was extensive and covered me as well.

"Are you going to give me a good show? Hm?" She questioned.

"Only if you give me one, first," I challenged, realizing what my wife had actually done for me.

As we stood chest to chest, the more the idea of someone joining us in bed resonated with me. My dick had hardened to the point of pain by the time she responded.

"Anything for you."

"I want her to make you cum while I watch."

"Only if you promise to fuck her from behind while she does."

"Laura," I pleaded.

"Then fuck another orgasm out of me," she replied, disregarding my objections.

"Okay," I grunted, loving the feeling of her fingers caressing my dick.

"Good boy," she praised, finally pulling me into the room with her and slamming the door behind us.

THREE

laura

I KNEW it would take some convincing on Liam's part, so when I was finally able to pull him into the room and introduce him to our friend for the night, my heart was doing backflips in my chest. Liam was a predictable lover and the best of them all. There was no doubt in my mind that he'd hesitate before accepting the fact that I'd brought someone into the bedroom with us.

However, I was just as sure that once the internal struggle was over, he'd perform well.

His selflessness was written all over his face after realizing what was going down tonight. I would bet my last dollar that he was worried about how I would feel or handle the sight of him entering another woman and giving her exactly what he'd been giving me all these years to make me bat shit crazy about him.

What he didn't understand was that I was looking forward to the very moment. Liam was the most committed father and husband I'd ever met in my life. I felt like he deserved a little fun, but only if I could oversee it. His stroke was deadly and I was desperate to see the look on another woman's face as she enjoyed every second of it.

I chuckled as he set the box he'd pulled from his pocket onto the table next to the door. He tilted his head to remind *me* that *he'd gotten me a gift for his birthday*. Tonight, he was in true Liam Eisenberg form. My husband never wanted the spotlight. Each year for his birthday he celebrated me. It was the weirdest, most pleasant thing ever, but this year it ended. I wouldn't allow it, so I hoped he adjusted well. This weekend would be his to have since he gave the other 51 or the year to me.

"I see it, baby," I assured him.

"It's an upgrade for the one you have," he said, excitedly.

Gifting the boys and me was the highlight of his days.

"I can't wait to see it... Monday."

"Monday?" He saddened.

"Clothes off, Liam," I demanded, needing him to focus. "Dick out."

I wasn't sure who the woman was that was speaking, tonight, but it wasn't Laura Eisenberg. The softness of my tone had been replaced with rigidness and the brown of my eyes had blackened. I was on a mission to please my husband tonight and I'd be damned if anyone stopped me – even him.

"Alright. Alright. Alright," he surrendered.

I watched closely as he stripped down to his boxers before turning toward me, again. This time, the uncertainty in his eyes was replaced by a burning desire. A smile crossed my lips as I approved the transformation before my eyes.

"You want to introduce me to our friend so that she can tell me her name before I stuff my dick in her mouth?" He asked.

"Joslyn," our guest spoke, causing Liam's attention to shift gears.

With a nod, he accepted her presence in the room. Before moving another muscle, he turned in my direction and placed hands on both sides of my face. Looking me square in the eyes, he softened.

"I love you, woman. You know that?"

"Ummm hmmm."

"Good. Understand that tonight means nothing. She means nothing. But, while she's here, I fully intend to fuck the shit out of her. Can't let the moment go to waste, right?"

"Nope," I responded with a smile, "I fully intend to enjoy every second of it, too."

"You better, because it's the first and final time you're bringing another woman into our bedroom so don't even think of trying this shit again."

"I won't," I promised.

"On your knees, sweetie," Liam called out to Joslyn.

She nearly leaped from the bed, happy to oblige. Her Hershey's colored skin was flawless, glistening under the dimness of the room. I was almost envious of her perfectly round eyes, extremely flat stomach, lack of waist for real, and the perky rack that sat on her chest. I wanted Liam to suck them both while he filled her belly with his long, veiny pole.

My husband's dick sprang from his boxers as he dropped them to the floor. Though it was a sight I'd had the privilege of seeing over and over again, it never got old. With a smirk that stretched across my face, I marveled at his light brown thickness.

Joslyn, on her knees in front of him, placed a hand on each of his thighs as he guided himself into her mouth. With a tilted head for a better view, Liam began to slowly fuck her throat. The lines that proved there was life in his body ran along his hands, letting me know that he was just as pleased as I was watching him indulge.

"That's right. Swallow this dick," he coached.

I admired my husband's beauty as I moved closer to the bed. In an attempt to not miss a second of the action, I kept my face forward and stepped backward until the back of my legs hit the mattress. Then, I lowered my body, resting my ass on the cold sheets. My left leg rose slowly until it was planted on top. With my index finger, I slid my g-string to the side to expose my warm, pink flesh.

As on queue, Liam's eyes reached me. His teeth pierced his bottom lip as he observed. Using my index and middle fingers, I applied pressure to my swollen clit. Its slipperiness wasn't a surprise to me. Watching Joslyn suck Liam's dick as if her life depended on it was all the motivation I needed for self-lubrication. My honey pot was dripping.

I twirled my wrist so that my fingers were in a constant, circular motion to bring as much pleasure to my clit as possible. The amount of saliva that Joslyn was able to conjure was appalling. Liam's dick was covered in her oral secretions. Everything began to be just a bit much for me, forcing me to close my eyes due to overstimulation. My sensitivity level was off the meter.

"Open your eyes." I heard Liam call out to me.

"Baby," I hissed.

"Now," he demanded.

I forced my lids apart and stared back at his handsome face. The sight of him drew my peak closer. My legs began to tremble as my fingers sped in pace. My vision aligned with Liam's center. His length disappeared and then reappeared and then repeated the process. Though Joslyn couldn't accommodate all of him, she managed to get most of him down her throat.

"Let it go," he grunted. "Let that shit go."

And, I did. I came so hard and for so long that I was seeing stars underneath my eyelids that I had no choice but to close at that point. My stomach caved and then expanded, over and over. My abdomen muscles tightened from the flexing of my body as I mounted and then began to come down from the euphoric height I'd reached.

"That's it, baby girl."

Liam's voice was closer this time. The heat of his body hovered over me, forcing my eyes open. To my surprise, I found him standing in front of me, massaging his dick as he pushed my g-string over just a little more. Before I could protest, he was sliding his wet dick inside of me.

"Fuck," Liam spat once he touched rock bottom.

Instinctively, my hands gripped his arms as I opened for him completely. While he adjusted to my snugness, I tightened my pussy muscles.

"Not fair," he mumbled before wrapping his right hand around my neck.

Just like that, he fucked me. With ease, he slid in and out. My pussy was sloppy and he was enjoying every second of it.

"Lay down," he commanded.

Joslyn found the space right next to me and lay down.

"Spread your legs."

She followed his orders, not missing a beat.

"Play with that motherfucker," he insisted.

The sight of her fingers rubbing her pretty pink flesh was one I'd never forget. Liam didn't let her have too much fun for too long or alone. He removed his dick from my oasis and slowly, carefully entered hers. I melted at the sight of my husband pleasing another woman. And, the look on Joslyn's face had me in a trance. She wasn't prepared for all that Liam had to offer and it took three positions and several retries for her to fully adjust. But, after a while, she managed.

We sucked and fucked and explored one another for over an hour. By the time Liam was releasing his seeds into my canal, we were all spent and ready for a good night's rest. Joslyn began gathering her belongings and before I could stop her, Liam did.

"Stay til morning," he said, taking the words right out of my mouth.

I'd enjoyed every bit of her and didn't mind one more round before we parted forever.

"Is that okay with you, Laura?" She asked, respecting my marriage and my boundaries.

Joslyn was aware of who Liam and I were and the extent of our relationship. She knew that we were a happily married couple who simply wanted a little fun for one night. There was nothing more to it, so another round of what we'd all just experienced was a very easy *yes* for me.

Instead of a verbal response, I patted the bed beside me. She was welcome to stay a little while longer, but after we had our fun with her in the morning she could leave immediately. Until then, everyone needed to get some shut-eye.

liam + laura

OUR INVITATION TO stay a little while longer wasn't in vain. The second I opened my eyes and felt Liam's hard dick on my legs, excitement filled me. On side of me was a still half, asleep Joslyn, whom's hand rested on my thigh. She laid flat on her back, giving me access to her clit. I placed my thumb against it and began rotating it until she was fully alert.

Joslyn quickly gathered her bearing. Eager to please me, she maneuvered in the bed until she was on all fours and her head was lodged between my legs. Her tongue swiped my clit once, twice, and then a third time. There wasn't a fourth. Instead, she latched onto my pussy and sucked my clit into her mouth.

"Shiiiiiiiiit," I gasped. She was truly gifted and understood the task well.

I reached over and wrapped my hand around as much of Liam's girth as possible. He was rock solid, watching Joslyn eat my insides out. Wanting to get in on the action, he placed my left breast in his mouth. However, I had other plans for him. I wanted him to get his dick wet. While he watched me, I wanted to watch him, too.

"Put it inside of her. Fuck her," I pleaded. "Fuck her."

Obliging, Liam gave my nipple a final peck before getting on his knees. I observed every move he made, intently, up until he entered Joslyn from behind. And, just like that, my orgasm hit me like a sack of bricks.

"Fuuuuuuuuuuuck. I'm cumming."

FOUR

liam

"POPS!" Laike shouted, raising his voice at me for the first time since he'd been living.

Though it made my blood boil, it brought me back to reality, which I was thankful for. That night had replayed in my head for years and years after it had happened but after a while, I thought it was behind me. Now, thirty-five years later, it was back to bite me in the ass. My line of vision blurred, slightly, as my emotions caught up to me.

Laura's face was the only one I wanted to see for now. And, there she was. Right in front of me with a weariness I'd only seen on her face twice – the first and second time she was diagnosed with cancer. That shit left a stain on my heart that I'd never be able to scrub off. This day was no different. With only my eyes, I apologized a million times in a matter of seconds.

"Pops!" Laike shouted, again, frustrating me.

"Make that the first and last time you raise your voice at me," I chastised.

"This nigga out here saying he's your son and all you're worried about is me raising my voice? My nigga, you've got some explaining to do!"

The sound of my front door opening made it easier to ignore my son. He was just as much in his feelings as I was in mine. However, there was no need for the hostility and anger that he was spewing. I was just as new to the situation as he was.

As the lanky, dark figure approached beside Luca, my oldest boy, I nearly lost my balance. My knees weakened as my heart nearly slowed to a complete stop. The two were splitting images, each of them adopting their mother's skin and eye colors.

Thirty-five years. My heart ached something awful thinking about how much time I'd missed of this boy's life. I couldn't imagine meeting Luca or Laike or Lyric at thirty-five. It would crush me, just like this. We deserved one another, no matter how difficult the situation or the circumstances. I deserved to know my boy. He deserved to know his father. My children were my pride and joy. He would've been, too.

And, though I'd just met him, I loved him immensely and immediately. I could see so much of myself in those dark eyes of his. From his cheekbones to his forehead, that was all me. I was staring back at a dark-skinned Liam. It was a scary sight.

"I'm Ledge," he said, extending a hand.

His politeness reminded me of his mother. From the jump, I could see that she'd done a good job raising him.

"Liam," I responded, pulling him in for a hug instead.

"Really?" Laike hissed.

"Shut up, nigga," Luca gritted, "This ain't bout you right now."

"Na. It's not. It's about this cheating ass

nigga here," Laike growled before pushing past us all.

"What?" Lyric's angelic voice shouted.

My heart broke, again, at the sound of it.

"This nigga got another kid, Lyric," Laike informed her.

"What?" She yelled, again, still confused.

Trying my hardest to stay focused, I tuned out the background noise and focused on the man in front of me. The man I knew nothing about. The man that I'd made in unison with my wife one night we decided to have a little fun. The man who had missed the opportunity to be a part of my family. The man whose life I'd missed the opportunity to be a part of.

"My mother died six months ago of a blood clot. It was sudden and unexpected. I finally went to her crib to clean it out... ya know. Finally able to deal with it all. I stumbled across this letter in a lock box she'd left for us that was full of memories from our childhood on up. I never even knew it existed until yesterday.

"Sorry to impose the way that I have, but I've wanted a father all my life. Knowing that he was in the same city and a few miles away, I couldn't just sit on that information. I had to come to see for myself after I read the note. I tried to get my brother, Lawe, to join me but he never cared who our father was. His anger suggests otherwise, though. I think it stems from not having you around."

"Brother?" Laike took the words right out of my mouth.

"Meaning like an entire side family right up under our noses?" Lyric followed, "Okay, wow. This is far too much for me right now. Where's my husband? I can't with this right now. Keanu!"

"Right behind you, sis," Laike hissed.

Luca, on the other hand, stayed put. Just like him, I was too stunned to move. *Brother?*

When the door finally slammed behind Laike and Lyric, I snapped out of it.

"Brother?" I questioned.

"We're twins."

liam + laura

WE'RE TWINS. The words replayed over and over in my head as I dialed Lyric's number for the fourth time in the last week. It was the longest I'd ever gone without speaking to her and it was eating me alive. I placed the phone up to my ear, only to listen to it ring out as I placed the glass of Remy to my lips.

Twins. Laike was up next. I'd called him about the same amount of times just to get ignored each time. The phone didn't even ring on his end. It went straight to voicemail each time. I assumed he had blocked my calls and texts. The thought of him being so angry without knowing the details of the situation saddened me.

The fact that he'd never know the details if it meant saving his mother some heartache and shame was a big pill to swallow but it was an easy one. I'd take the blame and the heat that they were tossing my way. I didn't mind going into the fire for Laura because I knew that she'd do the same for me without a doubt.

Besides, this was as much her fault as it was mine. I should've been a little more careful. The only explanation for the twins was the next morning when I re-entered Joslyn without cleaning myself properly. Sperm was viable for days after it hit the surface. Had I known then what I know now, this never would have happened. However, I wasn't at all regretful of my sons. I'd bring them into my circle and love them as they'd been in my life forever. It was the pain I caused the three

children I'd raised from babies that I was regretful of.

A full week without hearing either of
their voices or seeing their faces was torture
that my heart and head simply couldn't
stand. I ended the call to Laike and called the
one person I could count on to pick up for
me. In it all, he'd never left my side and I
doubted he ever would.

"What's shaking old man?" Luca
answered.

"Shit. Shit. You talked to those knotty
head-ass siblings of yours," I asked with a
heavy sigh that followed.

"Yeah. Yesterday."

"What they on?"

"Nothing much. Laike still seething and
Lyric won't stop whining. She's afraid the
twins are younger than her which would
make her belief that she was the baby all
these years untrue."

I chuckled. That was just like Lyric. She
took being the baby of the family to heart. It
was part of her identity.

"She ain't got to worry about that. Them
boys were conceived before she was a pea in
her mother's belly."

"Yeah. That's cool but I'm not telling her
that. I'm not opposed to her suffering right

57

now. Laike's either, especially knowing how they're handling you."

"It's alright son. But, I do think I owe it to you to tell you that I've never cheated on your mother. Ever. The thought has never even crossed my mind. Some shit just happens and then you look up wondering how the fuck it happened. That's where I am, now."

"I know, Pops. I know."

"Well, I'm going to let you go. Have you talked to him, again?"

"Yeah. I was trying to wait until Laike got out of his feelings to plan a meet-up. Just us boys, maybe Lawe, too?"

"From the sound of things, neither he nor Laike will be at that meeting," I sighed.

"Yeah. Wishful thinking. I'll set something up for next week with just the three of us, then, I imagine."

"Thanks, son."

"I love you. Don't be worried about those two spoiled ass kids of yours. They'll get it together. If they take too long, I'll have to pay them a visit."

"You and me both."

FIVE

laura

LIAM WAS A PILE OF SADNESS. It had been nearly two weeks since Ledge's visit and our two youngest still weren't talking to him. He'd called them several times and even stopped by their homes. His efforts were in vain. I watched as he pulled the white shirt over his head in preparation for bed. It was only eight, which was rather early for us both.

"So soon?" I asked, watching with a battered heart.

"Can I ask you something?" he said to me.

"Anything, Liam."

I meant it, too. He could ask me anything in the world and receive a response. That had always been the case and it would never change.

"Are you okay?"

It was just like him, always worried about me and my feelings. Here lately, though, I was the one worried about his feelings. Watching him crumble due to our children's refusal to communicate or acknowledge him while I knew the truth about the entire ordeal was a lot to handle. But, like a champion, he stood behind me and my decision to bring a woman into our bedroom all these years later.

With grace, he took the blame for a situation that I'd put us in. As a result, our children were turning their backs on him though it was me they should be upset with me. To protect me, he kept his lips sealed. As much as I appreciated it, I wanted to protect him this time.

"I'm fine, Liam. I have no regrets. I have no issues with how we're going to proceed.

Welcoming two boys into our world after being given a second chance at life is a blessing for me. They've lost their mother, unexpectedly, yet I'm still living and breathing. I'm going to be exactly what I am to the children we share with the ones we just got. I'm an Eisenberg, baby. Through and through. We're in this together. My heart hurts knowing that we missed so much of their lives... that's my only hiccup. I don't understand why she didn't reach out to us at some point."

"He gave me a letter that she wrote us both. I only got through the first paragraph before I realized none of it mattered anymore. All that matters now is how we move forward."

"What did the first paragraph say?"

"That she didn't want to disrupt our marriage. She loved the way that we loved one another and wanted us to spend the rest of our lives continuing to do so. Says she watched from afar and looked to us for hope. We helped her to understand that true, healthy Black love existed. So, to contribute to it, *to us*, she decided against sharing the pregnancy news, thinking it would crumble our foundation."

"It wouldn't have."

"I know. She didn't, though. Apparently, she felt as if she'd be the reason we split."

"Noooo. That wouldn't have happened."

"Not in this lifetime, but she didn't know that."

"I feel so bad, Liam. She had to raise them alone and now she's gone. There's no way to apologize or repay her or just..."

"I know, Laura. The only way we can make things right is by taking care of the boys from now on. Just because they're adults doesn't mean they don't need us. Luca, Laike, and Lyric still need us."

"You're right. Can I admit something?"

"Yeah."

"Twins? I'm over the moon about this. A little achy, yes, but more than anything I feel so blessed."

"Me, too. I'm happy as hell and sad at the same time. It's the weirdest shit, but I'm just taking the feelings as they come."

"You're really going to bed," I chuckled.

"Yeah. Not feeling that well," he grunted as he climbed into bed and underneath the covers.

He was suffering from a broken heart. It was affecting his emotional, mental, and physical health in the process. Liam was visibly ill due to Lyric and Laike's disappearance.

"Alright. I'm going downstairs. If you need me, buzz me."

"I'm headed to bed, Laura. I won't be needing anything."

"Goodnight," I responded, turning off the light near the door that I was preparing to walk out of.

"Goodnight."

liam + laura

AN HOUR HAD PASSED since I'd left Liam upstairs to rest his head and his heart, yet I wasn't any closer to sleep myself. Dressed fully with a Louis Vuitton fanny on my waist, I exited our home through the garage. As I pressed the button to raise the garage, I silently praised God for the silencer that Laike had installed when he remodeled it. Otherwise, Liam would be awake and downstairs before I was able to get my truck out.

The whimpering of our four-legged fur baby caused me to turn in the direction of the door that led to our kitchen. King, Luca's dog that we were only supposed to have for a few months while they adjusted to Elle's presence, was sitting next to it with desperation written all over his chunky face.

"Come on," I whispered as I opened the door for him to climb into my truck.

Once he was situated, I slid in after him. In a few seconds, I was out of the garage and out of the driveway. My wheels didn't stop turning until I was in front of Lyric and Ken's home. I left King inside as I exited the truck and headed up the walkway. Before I got the chance to ring the doorbell, Ken was at the door.

"Is everything straight? Is everybody straight? Come in."

"I'm fine right here. Everyone is okay, except Liam. Now, call your wife to the door so that I can have a few words with her."

"Is everything okay?" He asked, again.

"It will be when you get Lyric to the door."

"Alright."

He backed up and into the house further, but his eyes were still on me. It wasn't until he had to that he turned around and headed in Lyric's direction. When he returned, he wasn't alone. Lyric was at his side, wrapping her body in a robe with perplexity scribbled across her face.

"Mom, is everything alright?"

"When has your father ever let you down?" I questioned, propping a hand on my hip.

"Is this what this is about? Him?"

"Him has a fucking name!" I exclaimed, refusing to allow her to disrespect her father in my presence. Enough of that had gone on over the last two weeks. It ended, now.

"Really? You're using words like that when you talk to me, now?" Appalled, she asked.

"Grow the fuck up and answer my question, Lyric."

I was beyond the soft-natured Laura that everyone was used to because when it came down to my husband I would be the very monster he'd taught me to be. I didn't give a damn who caught my wrath, children included.

"Oh... wow," she scoffed.

"I'm waiting."

"Never," she answered.

"And, this situation is no different."

"He has TWO children. And, instead of checking him, you're at my doorstep? This man has an entire family outside of us. That's unforgivable. He's not the man I've known him to be all of these years. To save us both some time, energy, words, and gas, stay home next time."

"I thought sheltering you was a good thing all these years but I'm beginning to realize it's made you a very ditzy broad. Back in the day, I hated your type. Knows everything without knowing a damn thing. If for once you think that I'd stand behind a man that has cheated on me, you must be smoking the shit your husband is selling."

"Our husbands," she corrected.

"That, too." I shrugged.

"No one is innocent here."

"Oh, but your father is! See, he's willing to take the blame for this fiasco so that my name stays clean, but I'm unable to stand by while you and Laike crucify him and tarnish his character. He's not to blame here."

"How so? He's the one that stuck his di–penis in places it didn't belong."

"Actually, I did. I brought another woman into our bedroom and risked our future for a little fun. In 84, for your father's birthday, I orchestrated a threesome that involved Ledge's mother."

"That explains him but what about his

brother? Dad must've been dipping in it again."

"They're twins," I explained.

Her brows rose before falling just as quickly after she realized just how fucked up the entire situation was.

"So, don't feel sorry for me. Feel sorry for your father. Or don't. We're both happy to welcome Ledge and Lawe into our worlds. You'd better get on board or I'm at your door every day until you do. This family will not be divided because you and your brother can't get over yourselves. Neither Ledge nor Lawe nor Liam is to blame. If you want to be mad at someone, be mad at me. But, your father, he's off limits. I will fuck y'all worlds up if you keep fucking with him. Try me and see."

With that, I left a stunned Lyric at her door and climbed back into the truck. I ended the journey in Laike's driveway. Luckily, he had just pulled in himself. Before I could even begin to speak, he was already waving me off.

"Not tonight," he slurred, obviously having had one too many drinks.

As I silently thanked God for his safety, I made my way toward his car. He posted up against it with his hands folded over his chest.

When I reached him, I was a little more disgusted than I imagined I would be.

"Your father has been calling you."

"Fuck that nigga," he spat with a smug look on his face.

Long before I was able to comprehend what was happening, my open hand landed on his face.

SMACK!

"Get your shit together and don't ever fix your mouth to speak about your father that way. That man has been nothing but a blessing to us all. He deserves far more credit than you're giving him right now!"

"We're on that now? Putting your hands on me?"

Tears welled in Laike's eyes, breaking my heart in the process. I felt hot, thick tears hit my cheeks as I realized what I'd done. I'd never put my hands on my children, even in their youth. They were decent kids and there was nothing a little verbal lashing couldn't correct.

"I'm trying to slap some fucking sense into you, son," I cried, "Your father has never stepped out on me. I'll have you understand that first. It was me. I did this to us. I tried to be spontaneous and invite a woman into our bed. He didn't support it but went along with it because his entire world revolves around me... us... always has. So, he went along with it. Unfortunately, these are the results.

"Twins. And, as much as society would want me to be upset about it... I'm not. I love the idea of having the boys. I've always wanted more children but after Lyric, my uterus ruptured and children were no longer an option for me. That's why I spend my days around children and love the thought of either of you giving me more.

"Laike, it's not his fault. It's mine. Be mad at me, son, but don't treat him like this. He's worried sick. You can't do this to him."

"I didn't know," he huffed, tears streaming down his handsome face.

"You didn't try to find out. You didn't give him the benefit of doubt. You just believed the worst of a man who has only shown us time and time again who he is. It's not the man you painted him to be these last two weeks."

"That's what hurt the most... knowing that wasn't the man who'd raised me."

"It's not. The person he's shown you he is your entire life is who he truly is."

"I'm sorry," he apologized.

"Don't tell me. I'm not the one you owe the apology to. Tell him."

I left him with those words and hopped back into the truck with one more destination in mind before I headed home. Less than six minutes away was Luca's home. When I pulled into the driveway, I watched him close the door behind him and sit on the porch. It was obvious he'd talked to one of his siblings. He was waiting for me, knowing I'd come.

"Which one was it?" I asked, smiling.

"Lyric."

"Figures."

"She called to tell me she's still the baby."

"Of course, that's all she got out of the conversation."

"Nah, she also got that you really a low-key freak and that's why we're here, now, with two new Eisenbergs."

I shared a hearty laugh with him while shaking my head.

"Actually, they're Dominos. They don't have our last name."

"Dominos?" Luca asked in deep thought.

"Yeah. That's their mother's last name."

"There are a few Dominos on our roster. You sure they're not related?"

"I wouldn't doubt it. I did my research, of course. It's a slew of them. Ledge and Lawe are part of a large family. Some very beautiful people. Did you see how smooth his skin was?"

"Gots to figure out that nigga's skincare routine," he chuckled.

"It's genetic. His mother's skin was just as smooth and delicate. She was a gorgeous woman. I'm not surprised her children are just as beautiful."

"You need to be getting home, old lady."

"I do. I just wanted to drop by and thank you for not turning your back on your father."

"Never. I could never do that."

"I know. I love you," I told him as I stretched my arms for a hug.

"Beyond measure," he responded, bringing comfort to my heart. It was a response his father sometimes gave.

"King is in the car," I said as I walked off.

"Let him out. He can spend some time with us. Lucas' badass misses him, anyway. All he talks about most days."

"Leave my baby alone."

King was excited to hop out once I opened the passenger door. He ran right up to Luca's porch and through the door that he held open for him.

liam + laura

WHEN I RETURNED HOME, I was unable to pull into the garage due to a very familiar car blocking the entrance. Laike's Mercedes was slanted in the driveway, an obvious sign that he was intoxicated. I didn't care much. As long as he made it safely and as long as he was inside making amends with his father, I was satisfied.

I was expecting to see the father and son pair in the common areas of the house. However, I couldn't find them anywhere, not even in Liam's man cave. I quickly gave up my search and ended up heading for our bedroom. Exhaustion and emotions were weighing me down. I was ready for bed.

What I walked into was far beyond my imagination. On either side of Liam lay Lyric and Laike. Both were in their pajamas with their shoes next to the bed. It was obvious that neither of them had intentions of leaving out, again. With a shake of my head, I removed my shoes and headed for the shower, trying my hardest not to disturb them.

"You're sleeping on the couch tonight. You're in trouble," Lyric hollered out.

"Sho is," Laike followed up.

"Leave her alone. I'll put y'all asses out of my bed before I put her out."

"See, that's the issue now. Y'all too invested!"

"Goals!" Lyric exclaimed. "Goals."

"When I get back, y'all might as well scoot on over. My husband says I'm sleeping right there tonight."

THE END.

The Domino Effect coming February 2023

Pre-Order Ledge now on Amazon.

LIAM'S NOTE

Liam here,

Just here to thank everyone who has been on this rollercoaster ride with my family and I. We're forever grateful. What you've had the pleasure of experiencing so far is only the beginning. There's something much bigger in store.

For those who doubted my love and loyalty to my family and to my wife, fuck you. I mean that in the most disrespectful way.

I'm out. The twins are up next.

Big L

HUFFINGTON NEWS

Join over 11,000 honorary Huffington residents for monthly broadcasts delivered right to their preferred devices.

Broadcasts include but aren't limited to:

- A beautiful monthly newsletter detailing everything happening in Huffington
- Extensive snippets of upcoming projects (sneak peeks)
- Release day reminders that include links (to remove the guest work from searching for books on Amazon/Ghuffington.com)
- First to hear about surprise releases
- Exclusive discounts + offers for Huffington residents
- A monthly wrap-up detailing everything that has happened in

Huffington since the release of
the Huffington Newsletter

Ready to become a resident?
Click here.
[https://huffingtonnews.ck.page/
4693a79283]

MORE FROM GREY HUFFINGTON

Find the entire collection of Grey Huffington titles below. Titles in the catalog are available in eBook (amazon.com, + ghuffington.com), paperback (ghuffington.com), or audiobook (audible + ghuffington.com) formats.

Syx + the City
Syx + the City 2
Syx Thirty Seven
Syxth Giving
Syx Whole Weeks

Wilde + Reckless
Wilde + Relentless
Wilde + Restless

Mr. Intentional
Unearth Me

The Sweetest Revenge
The Sweetest Redemption

Half + Half
The Emancipation of Emoree

Sleigh
Sleigh Squared

The Gifted
Memo
Give her Love. Give her Flowers.

Unbreak Me
Uncover Me

As we Learn
As we Love

Just Wanna Mean the Most to You
Sensitivity
10,000 Hours
Darke Hearts
muse.

Softly
Peace + Quiet
Press Rewind
Jagged Edges

My Person
The Realm of Riot Thimble
Whose Love Story is it Anyway?
Unhand Me

Home*
Blues*
31st*
Now That We're Here.*

Then Let's Fuck About It*
Giving Thanks

A Month of Sundays Ep 1
A Month of Sundays Ep 2
A Month of Sundays Ep 3
Dinner at Ever + Luca's
Saylah
The Mayor's Ball
Elm

THE EISENBERG EFFECT

Luca
Lyric
Ever*
Laike
Baisleigh*
Liam

THE DOMINO EFFECT

Ledge
Halo*
Lawe
Kleuless*

BERKELEY BRED

Malachi
Anna*
Milo
Makai
Glacier*
Mercer
Vallei*

THE GREY LIST

Chemistry
"The Chemist"
Egypt
Rather
"The Therapist"
Priest
Rugger
"The Huntress"
Psalms
Roulette
"The Madam"
Israel
Rome

"The Ballerina"
Saint

--

* signifies the publication is available
EXCLUSIVELY on ghuffington.com.

--

Prefer Audiobooks?

Did you know **there's a library FULL
of audiobooks on ghuffington.com**
for the lovers who listen?

Audiobooks Available (**exclusively on
GHuffington.com**)

Egypt
Ever
Baisleigh
Halo
Kleuless
Anna
Glacier
Vallei
Elm.
And more

www.ingramcontent.com/pod-product-compliance
Lightning Source LLC
Chambersburg PA
CBHW010933120626
46552CB00009B/3231